MY RHYMES FOR REASONS

We are as gifts unwrapped within our allotted time
A present to ourselves locked in our cautious minds
Without a cause at life's beginning
We chase around losing and winning
For this is life and all its ways
From our first light till dying day
And so if I may please
Within these pages I will conceive
For you what I have dreamt and here will bring
They will describe my finest offerings
Of days of love of hate of winter and of spring
I'll speak of all my many savored seasons
Till you are drenched of all my thoughts
I offer you My Rhymes for Reasons.

MY RHYMES
FOR
REASONS

WOLRAD

First Edition Wolrad Press

© WOLRAD (Mark Darlow) 2019, All rights reserved.

Wolrad Press
710 West End Avenue, Suite 10A
New York, NY 10025-6808
E-mail: mhdarlow@gmail.com

Books may be purchased in quantity
by contacting the publisher directly.

ISBN Print: 978-0-9890144-2-7
ISBN E-book: 978-0-9890144-3-4
Library of Congress Control Number: 2019903220

Edited: Sheldon Darlow
Interior Design: Steve Kennedy
Front/Back Cover Design: Andrew Darlow
Photographs: The photographs contained in this publication may not be reproduced in whole or part by any means whatsoever without written permission from the copyright owner (Andrew Darlow).

DEDICATION

I dedicate this collection of rhymes/poems to my family and friends. Especially my loving wife, older brother and children. They have truly inspired me throughout my life. I've always tried, with an open heart, not to miss an occasion or holiday. I hope that those who have received my rhymes have felt the heartfelt sincerity they are written to express. For this opportunity, I am sincerely thankful.

TABLE OF CONTENTS

10 *A New Friend*

12 *Where Would We Be?*

14 *My Pen Pal*

16 *Your Hat is Still There*

18 *The Making of a Sonnet*

20 M & A

22 *Jump Right In*

24 *Now That You're Gone*

26 *Words Forever*

28 *The Only Thing Missing*

30 *Heaven Needed Our Piano Man*

32 *Pain's Challenge*

34 *The Eight Syllable Sonnet*

36 *The Ten Syllable Sonnet*

38 *Whatever It Takes*

40 *The Torture of Time*

42 *The Ravages of War*

44 *I'm Not Sure*

46 *Brick By Brick*

48 *St. Patrick and The Giant*

52 *A Golden Haired Beauty*

54   *Finding Love*

58   *Why Not Eat Worms*

60   *Scared Silly*

62   *Swan Lake*

64   *Because*

66   *I Just Got Bit*

68   *Reflect*

70   *The Race Is On*

72   *Careful Young Hearts*

74   *My Dream*

76   *Resolve*

78   *Before I Close My Eyes*

80   *Seasons*

82   *Family*

84   *Don't Hide*

86   *Is There Really More Than This?*

88   *Something Special*

92   *I Love My Father So*

94   *Are We Remiss*

96   *Why Do I Love Thee?*

98   *In Closing*

THE HISTORY OF WOLRAD

My name is Mark Howard Darlow, though as you can see, my poetry/rhymes are signed Wolrad, a name I've inscribed on all I've written.

Wolrad is the name my father, Nathaniel Hawthorne Darlow, created by spelling our name Darlow backward. He called himself Tan Wolrad, Nat Darlow in reverse. I decided as a young writer/poet that I also would carry the torch forward and use Wolrad as my pen name. I know my father would be proud to see his namesake, his nom de plume, in print on these pages.

So, you will see the Wolrad signature at the bottom of every poem, along with the year it was written. This is in keeping with the memory of my father. Wolrad lives on my every page.

INTRODUCTION

I've written countless little thoughts and rhymes to people I have run into in all of life's circumstances. From strangers to my friends and family, though especially to people at bars and restaurants. I grab a napkin and quickly write a thought. It usually rhymes and always, well almost always, makes a nice impression.

I've learned through life that very few people have poems written for them. This small gesture often makes their day. Almost all the time, I don't rewrite them or keep a copy for myself. I do often put my email on the back and suggest they send me a copy. They usually never do.

I've noticed something that does seem consistent. When I run into the person, they often say "Hey you're the guy that wrote me that poem. I have it on my refrigerator". Funny, but true. You never know when putting yourself out there for people to judge you, how they will react. Regardless, I have been doing this for over 40 years and will till, well you know when.

You will also see some of the many holiday and birthday cards I've created, and some of the sad memories when close friends and family leave us.

My hope is that you enjoy all the emotion that I've brought to these poems. How often I laughed and too often cried as I finished that last line. That line always brings out the reason for the rhyme.

A NEW FRIEND

This is a poem I wrote for a lady bartender at the Azure restaurant in the Renaissance Hotel on 38th Street in Manhattan. My son, Matthew, had invited my wife and I, along with his girlfriend for Valentine's Day 2019. This mixologist was so excited about the first napkin poem I wrote her, I wrote this one right after.

By the way, she makes a great Dirty Vodka Martini. I took a picture with my cell phone so I would remember it.

Fortune is when
You've made a new friend
Someone to talk to
Regardless of when
There is nothing better
When letters won't do
A friend is that someone
Who will always come through.

WOLRAD/2019

WHERE WOULD WE BE?

I had the extreme honor to be presented with the John Peter Zenger Medal for my humanitarian efforts over the years.

Back in 1774, Zenger, the publisher of his family weekly newspaper, The New York Weekly Journal, wrote satirical stories about the then Governor of New York, William Cosby. Zenger constantly pointed out Cosby's corruption and profiteering policies. The Governor made attempts to stop the stories, to no avail. Cosby then had Zenger arrested and locked up in the local jail.

After a lengthy trial that lasted almost a year, Zenger was acquitted. The court agreed that if a person writes or speaks the truth, and can prove in to be factual, he should not be held against his will. This led to the first known case of Freedom of the Press.

A little-known fact: While John Peter Zenger was in jail, his wife ran the newspaper and never missed a deadline.

I was awarded the medal at the Franklin/Luminaire's annual dinner in 2016. At the end of my acceptance speech, I recited this poem.

It is 1774 when we start this historic tale
We find John Peter Zenger locked up in jail
His satirical attacks on William Cosby
 the then governor of the state
Did not think his stories in
 The New York Weekly Journal
  were too great
He confined Mr. Zenger for almost a year
Until his lawyers made it extremely clear
You may write, publish or say all that is true
And the law shall not do anything to you
They convinced the jury it was clear all could see
And "Freedom of the Press" was decreed
Looking back almost 300 years
The courage of Zenger brings a chill and a tear
If it wasn't for he who would have changed history
Where would we be without John Peter Z?

WOLRAD/2016

MY PEN PAL

Pen Pals were a familiar part of many of our lives. So many of us older folks wrote letters to friends and family.

My father had a Pen Pal that he never spoke to. I once asked him; "How come you don't call her?" His answer was; "No...our relationship is in the letters we write back and forth. We are only Pen Pals".

When she passed away, her son called my dad to tell him that his letters meant so much to her. He said they were one of the most important moments in her life.

My sister also had a Pen Pal from London, England. Their relationship eventually grew to them meeting both in the U.S. and London. The letters made that friendship what it was. From hearing their stories and others I've known, I created this next piece.

I've lost my pen pal to the web
My lust for the written word is dead
Her quill's gone dry
Please tell me why
What will I take to bed
Within her thoughts
She always caught
The truth inside of me
How could this world I loved so well
Turn to catastrophe
Each envelope so well addressed
The smell alone I would caress
They took me places I could never go
If not for her I would not know
After all those lovely years
Of cheers of fears of tears
As I address this first e-mail
My heart's begun to cry
I feel as if this is the end
As if a sad goodbye
Her Spenserian loops that flowed so well
Are fonts on my screen so drab
The ink she used from pens of old
Would always show a dab
With her words the same
I'll play along with this game
Then print her letters to save
My pen pal is my e-pal now
And will be to my grave.

WOLRAD/2000

YOUR HAT IS STILL THERE

A close friend's father passed away. I knew him well. I would always send him birthday and holiday cards. He truly enjoyed them and would be so grateful that I never forgot him on these occasions, especially on his birthday.

He was 99 years old when he passed away, and so fortunate to have all his faculties about him at the end. This is the poem I wrote for his family and friends.

Your hat is still hanging on the wall in the hall
It's there where you left it ready on call
A little bit higher than the rest of our gear
When your hat was in place we all knew you were near
If I should remove it there would be a big hole
Like the one when you passed that's so icy cold
I can't seem to shake it that feeling remains
They say in some time I'll get back in the game
So it will remain hanging where it belongs
Each time that I pass it I'll think nothing's wrong
I'll recall as we gathered our coats and our hats
To walk from our home for this and for that
There are so many moments that began from that spot
So many times we said; "Forget me not!"
Why was the love of my life taken in a flash
I'd trade one more moment for all of my cash
For life has its partners that wear their hats well
My love of my life I'll continue to tell
I'll keep every dream every moment we spent
I'll never believe looking back they were lent
I thought we would live forever in love
As that picture we bought of two loving Doves
There's one hook still empty I've left on the wall
For family and friends and strangers all
As they leave I'll look up and always recall
Your hat that's still hanging there on the wall.

WOLRAD/2018

THE MAKING OF A SONNET

I've always loved writing Shakespearian Sonnets. The complex quest of completing the exact formula of rhyming lines and the exact count of ten syllables to a line. I've written this sonnet describing what makes up a proper ten syllable, fourteen-line Shakespearian Sonnet.

Throughout this book, I will add a variety of sonnets I've written and the reason that inspired me to create them.

First what makes up a Shakespearian Sonnet
A simple question with the answer forthwith
Think of costumes you wear with a Bonnet
Our look would be improper without it

There must be four lines three times and then two
Each of the four must rhyme every other
Then to complete you rhyme the last two
These lines combat as sister and brother

And of course there must be a story told
One that will always seek to discover
It may be filled with love if you be so bold
Or a simple prose without a lover

   You must decide then keep the word count true
   And each Sonnet you write will reflect you.

WOLRAD/2018

M & A

I've been very fortunate to have met an extremely talented Acupuncturist, who recently teamed up with another great talent in the field.

With techniques I've never seen before, they have helped me to resolve many issues that have plagued me in my life. The way they combine herbal medicine with their needling techniques is quite unique.

I wrote this poem as a thank you to them both. They framed it and hung it in their office. There's a few extra personal lines and my signature at the bottom. You will have to go to their office to see the inscription.

It takes a kind of chemistry
A synergy
A blend
When merging two gems together
Who's plan now sets the trend
The way they work in harmony
Fixing problems daily that they see
Leaves nothing left for guessing
As they solve life's mysteries
It's not just how they touch those spots
It's not just what they mix in pots
It's not just one specific thing
It's how they make your body sing
They never rush you out too soon
As they restore your life in tune
It's just as if they've used a broom
To sweep away your pain
If only there would be a way
To merge together those some day
Who've yet to learn their secret gifts
Too many think be thrift and skip
And so I say with heartfelt thanks
You've saved me from that old ship's plank
I know now from this moment on
My mind and body will again be strong.

WOLRAD/2019

JUMP RIGHT IN

I was sitting around with my three best friends. We've known each other for the better part of our lives. There's nothing we haven't said or can't say to each other that would not be taken in friendship. One of the guys, as all of us, is getting old and feeling it. He started complaining, which then put me to work later that day writing this poem.

Stop saying things you don't believe
Jump right in roll up your sleeves
The water's fine it's not too cold
It keeps your bones from getting old
Is it not true you wish it be
Back when you were just twenty-three
When life was what life was meant to be
Young and strong building history
So your bones ache
For heaven's sake
You're old and you can't stand up straight
It is I'm told in nature's plan
You grow up get old and lose your tan
It does not make you less a man
Relive those days when skies were blue
You worked too hard not to follow through
Jump in the water's fine and cool
That's how my friend we'll remember you.
WOLRAD/2012

NOW THAT YOU'RE GONE

As you can imagine, or will imagine, I have written many poems for those who are grieving for a close person who recently passed away. This was written specifically for someone who was very close to my wife and later became a close friend to me.

Zigmund (Ziggy) Galko died from cancer. It happened so quickly, my wife and I felt we never had the chance to say the kind of things you would say to a close friend at that time.

I created this poem for her. I removed his name when I rewrote the piece. I have since sent it to many people over the years. I've been told that it has been read at funerals.

I cannot tell you how I feel
   now that you're gone
My feelings fill the room
   there's so much wrong
I want to hold my breath
   and be so strong for you
No matter how I try
   this I cannot do
You were my friend and confidant
   so many times before
This space cannot be filled
   not now or evermore
For in my dreams the character
   that saved me from the dark
Is just a shadow as if a tree has lost its leaves
   and stands just bark
Forgive me I have not the strength to hold my head
   this day erect
My thoughts reject the news
   that you have passed
At last what wanders in and out my head
   can't be
I'm sorry at the end I never told you
   how much you meant to me
For what is life when those are taken
   in a moments glance
And all that's left are loving souls
   to claim a second chance.

WOLRAD/2012

WORDS FOREVER

My older brother, Sheldon, my closet friend and the editor for this rhyming poetry book, is also a poet.

We are continuously writing back and forth, sending our poems along. We both have been creating Shakespearian style sonnets for years.

I wrote this sonnet for him after he had sent me one of his best works to date. The title should be "Love Forever".

A sonnet that serves a purpose no less
Your best my bro has yet been imagined
You put me and all the others to test
And leave us amazed with the biggest grin

For there may be many others who write
That is their life's purpose there is no doubt
Let them read this one and go fly a kite
They can't win this lifelong creative bout

Soon the whole universe will know the truth
If they will sit and read what you have scribed
Writing prose should have been your game since youth
They will know now that I've taken your side

    Why are words written if not to be rhymed
    And be read by all forever in time?

WOLRAD/2018

THE ONLY THING MISSING

My Aunt Sylvia, who was also my godmother, my mother's youngest sister, and the last of the original Benzer family, was in her last days.

My cousin gave her an iPad to use while in a hospice facility. I was writing her emails and sending, what I call, "The Thought for The Day Is…". This is the Thought for The Day I attached to the last email I sent to her.

She passed away soon after. I'll never forget what my cousin said to me when she called to tell me she had passed away. "A world without Aunt Sylvia."

As the weather turns warm
   and the flowers appear
I gaze out my window
   and cheer with a tear
The beauty surrounds me
   I'm lost in the view
The only thing missing
   is you.
           WOLRAD/2011

HEAVEN NEEDED OUR PIANO MAN

A very close friend just lost her father. I knew him well and always thought him to be a terrific guy.

As I write this, it is only a couple of weeks since he passed away. He was an accomplished jazz pianist who played with the best.

He was also a coach in high school. He could kick a football as well any anyone in the pros. A little info many don't know. If you punt a football with your left foot, the ball spins in a way making it harder to catch.

His daughter and close friend always said, "My dad's left foot kicking made it almost impossible to catch."

There must have been a spot that opened
    in Gabriel's Band
That couldn't be filled by
    just any man
They needed a guy who's piano
    had that sound
That gave you a lift
    when feeling low down
They needed the man
    who played with the best
That when in his youth
    he passed every test
When they searched all the towns
    and all the cool spots
It was Jack Bloomberg's name
    that rose to the top
That must be the reason
    what else could it be
The long football season
    had no need of he
All the kickers and punters
    were off till next year
It must have been Gabriel
    to me it's quite clear
Now that the Angels have a legend
    sitting at the keys
When heaven plays jazz they'll be
    grooving with ease
They'll be swinging to riffs
    as only our man can play
And we'll know that our Jack
    is making God's day.

WOLRAD/2019

PAIN'S CHALLENGE

Who doesn't have an issue with pain? It's either neck pain or arm pain or the most dreaded pain of all, Sciatica, when it starts at your lower back and runs down your leg.

I have suffered my share of pain from most of the common causes, just like you. One day I lifted something heavier than I should have from my closet. I felt that pull that you never want to feel. I was hoping it would go away by itself.

The next day I was off to my Chiropractor. In between, I meditated a few times a day. I'm not sure which worked better. The combination did the job in about two weeks.

Pain has many deep-set roots
Often tooting its blasting horn
Causing you those well-known aches
As if you've stepped upon a thorn
No use you just can't shake it
You've waked a sorry old wound
For only just this moment
Your whole life is out of tune
"So, what to do?" you ask yourself
As you try your best to rise
Above this place this endless race
You shutter to disguise
There is a light within you
Way down so deep your soul
That constantly releases you
From paying your pain's toll
Dig deeper than you have before
Begin by opening your minds door
Inside you'll find a burning flare
To challenge all that stings and dares
Turn 'round your ways begin your fight
Take on what pain does best
Within a day or maybe two
Pain's gone and you're at rest.

WOLRAD/2018

THE EIGHT SYLLABLE SONNET

Over the years, I've written many Shakespearian Sonnets. Always keeping to William's ten syllable fourteen-line format. The flow, or pentameter, has a rhythm to it that is distinctive in its own way.

I've noticed that I'm almost always forcing the ten syllable line. I seem to find an eight syllable style fits my style of writing more smoothly, with less effort.

As I wrote this, every line was exactly eight syllables. I didn't have to force anything. I wanted to share this experience with writers who, as I've noticed, never seem to worry about the syllable or line count in their sonnets. I'm not sure if that is because they are not aware of how sonnets were created, or not.

I'm extremely thankful that I do not represent the person I'm writing this sonnet about. The suffering broken heart can be either a gal or a guy.

You may notice I rhymed this sonnet with a different format. The first and forth line and the second and third line are rhymed. I like trying the different formats I've seen various poets use.

You broke my heart with just your thoughts
Tight lips gave way to times before
You broke me down to my life's core
We did not speak we had not fought

My soul reached out for just a glance
Please why did you now end this way
How will I go about my days
You've ended my life's true romance

I'll try for you have asked me so
To live my life without your love
My hands now reach to him above
As you now turn as you now go

I'll not again know love this real
In time I'll heal what you now steal.

WOLRAD/2019

THE TEN SYLLABLE SONNET

I've rewritten this sonnet using the Shakespearian ten syllable format. I had to force the extra two syllables to make the sonnet work out.

I wanted to make this point clear to my readers. In the future I will be exploring the many sonnet formats that have been used since the fifteenth century. This may take an entirely new poetry book dedicated only to sonnets.

You broke my heart with just a moments thought
Tight lips gave way to many times before
You've broken me way down to my life's core
We did not ever speak we had not fought

My soul reached out for just another glance
Please why did you now end our love this way
How will I ever go about my days
You have ended my life's only romance

I'll try for you have asked me to do so
To live life without your most precious love
My hands reach up in prayer to him above
As you now turn away as you now go

I'll not ever again know love this real
In time I know I'll heal what you now steal.

WOLRAD/2019

WHATEVER IT TAKES

Getting old isn't easy. I had just gotten off the phone with a close friend I've known the better part of my life. We both started in kindergarten together when we were just five years old. He was complaining of the same pains I have, and that remembering which pills to take and when to take them was becoming a difficult task.

After hanging up on him, I reflected our conversation in the following poem.

I used to study
　new found things
Now old problems
　have changed my ways
Yesterday I never dreamed
The way I'd feel today
I learned to line-up
　all those pills I take
How to stretch first thing
　so I won't ache
How to remember
　one thought to the next
How to learn
　all those cell phone tricks
　　and how to text
I think
　I'm getting better
　　though I'm not sure
　　　just where I'm at
At times I can't remember
　was it this
　　or was it that
If only they would
　make a pill
I'd welcome
　the new monthly bill
Whatever it takes
　I'm in all the way
That is my sacred promise
　till my final judgment day.
　　WOLRAD/2017

THE TORTURE OF TIME

Time, that cruel clock that never stops ticking. We want so much to be older when we are young. We say; "I can't wait to be 18 and be old enough to drive".

Always something that we want that takes being older. We keep wishing until we reach that point where we want the clock to reverse. We want to feel the way we used to when we were in our thirties, even our forties and fifties.

We can't hold back the hands of time. Old father time gets his due sooner or later.

As the years scratch away
At your skin and bones
And your daily pain adds to your groans
You bend
You lift
You want your gift of youth back again
Those promises now gone since then
Those places and races are all left behind
Your mind becomes blind
To your memory's past
Why didn't your youthful body last
Your life seemed staged you starred in the cast
You keep trying while crying
Give me one more chance to stop dying
You know there is nothing you can do
The torture of time
Relentlessly so
How were you to ever know?

WOLRAD/2019

THE RAVAGES OF WAR

*Watching TV these last twenty years has been a downer for
me, when they show our brave soldiers shooting weapons and
being shot at. When I hear about the casualties of the day or
the week or the current war.*

*I've often thought of many poems to write. This one, I feel,
brings out what I want the people of our planet to hear and
feel. Let us hope in the near future, we will find a way to stop
all this senseless killing of our young men and women.*

The ravages of war
It's anyone's guess
Who will be eating at the very next mess
Who will live to recall what they have done
Who will declare to the world they are number one
War doesn't know or see who you are
War doesn't know where you are
Divided by virtues dying for sins
Captains and Colonels fight till they win
War teaches techniques to keep soldiers alive
Always advancing stride after stride
Don't think turning back
Don't think you can hide
Don't love anyone that's not on your side
Nights in the trenches bring thoughts in the dark
Fires are burning just like home in the park
The war is asleep till the sun rises and then
Soldiers will die again and again.

WOLRAD/2017

I'M NOT SURE

After reviewing the last poem about war, I recalled when I did my hitch in the Army. I was a young 18-year-old who enlisted in the National Guard. At 18, I only had to serve six months of active duty and then a year and a half in the National Guard reserves.

My luck, along with the rest of the world, our friends the Russians decided to start trouble and move some of their missiles to Cuba. That created enough trouble, along with what was going on in Germany, for President Kennedy to freeze everyone in the service for another year.

I was one of the more fortunate ones to not have been pulled back in for a year of active duty. This poem reminded me of that time in my life.

I wake up every morning
Should I shower first or eat
There's always some confusion
As the floor and my feet meet
The thoughts keep running through me
I'm not sure of which comes first
I drink a glass of water
To quench my night long thirst
The rising sun begins to burst
Upon the morning scene
Which brings me to a long ago remembering
When I enlisted in the Army
They decided this for me
They woke me every morning
Told me exactly where to be
The day started with some stretching
The sun was coming up
I wanted for some coffee
Thick and black in my tin cup
With some beat up eggs and toast
All roasted to a tee
That was the kick each morning
That did the trick for me
Our Sergeant guided us throughout
Each long hard dreary day
We crawled and ran till the sun went down
"No time to frown!" he'd say
He molded us as if he was molding human clay
The best part of my hitch I still believe
Was what my new body did achieve
Now I'm still not sure this morning
As I open my eyes wide
Should I shower first or eat
Or pull the covers up and hide.

WOLRAD/2017

BRICK BY BRICK

I was sitting one day looking at my first home and recalling what it felt like as it was being built. I had decided to make the front all brick. It cost a little bit extra, though it made a huge difference in the overall look. I thought to myself; "Wow, my first home, how cool!".

I then recalled coming home from work the first night. The feeling I had as I drove up my driveway. You can't beat those memories, those emotions, they live with you forever.

Brick by brick its shape takes form
Day by day it grows
Strong enough to weather storms
For how long no one can know
Within its shell life will rejoice
Fate will be the judge each day
Those blessed will hear its inner voice
As it calls out "Be happy and please stay!"
The sun and rain and the winds will blow
From all four corners and above
Light will shine and water will flow
As it fills our home with peace and love.

WOLRAD/1999

ST. PATRICK
AND
THE GIANT

The following is a fable
that was written just for fun.
It tells about the biggest man
'twas said he weighed a ton.
St. Patrick was his favorite Saint
no man could take that away.
Each night he raised his glass in praise
to thank him for his day.

Once upon a time on the softest field of green
A bonnie lass stopped to rest knowing soon that she would bring
A baby lad so big they said how could it be just one
'Twas born without a problem underneath the rising sun

The lass took just one look and said it's John to be your name
Your father James Magee for your size I'm gonna blame
She took him to the tavern for the world to see her boy
To have a pint and raise a toast to this bundle full of joy

He grew to be the biggest man the world would ever know
They all believed the tales he told who wouldn't don't you know
He walked as tall you've ever seen a man could ever stride
The trees themselves if you believe all quickly stepped aside

Our hero was a gentle man on Sunday he would rest
In church to give praise and thanks to his Saint that was his best
A special spot was crafted for our man the size of two
With a place to set his feet upon within his giant shoes

As time went by our John Magee became someone fun to see
He told the grandest stories at the pub for pints and fee
He always made you laugh as he raised his glass and say
"St. Patrick put me on this earth and made me just this way!"

Our gentle John and though he was no man would say that name
Decided he would travel to the next town for a change
To see the world he's never seen and find himself a wife
But who would marry John Magee for sure would be for life

As fate would have it in that town just miles down the road
Our gentle fearsome giant found a woman don't you know
As big as he and beautiful to John she ever was
The moment that he saw her eyes his heart began to pause

They married at the church that John spent Sundays every week
Then built themselves the biggest house along a crooked creek
Within a year a child had come a size no one could dream
They named their son John Patrick for the blessings he did bring

Through the years they all believed the stories John would tell
Especially St. Patrick's tales he learned to tell so well
If ever there could ever be a man to spin a yarn
'Twas John about St. Patrick with his special kind of charm

Now just like every fairy tale this one must find an end
For men like John the giant are not the type to start a trend
Believe in what you wish my friend for wishes do come true
Like John Magee St. Patrick is also there for you.

WOLRAD/2000

A GOLDEN-HAIRED BEAUTY

So often I've noticed Golden Retrievers as seeing eye dogs on trains, buses or just walking in the streets. People are always looking at them. They know not to touch or handle them in any way. Still, just like me, they are always curious.

I wrote this while on a subway in Manhattan, sitting opposite a seeing eye dog and his owner. I made up the part about the Long Island Railroad train.

Each morning I see them on the 7:40 train
A beauty with golden hair and her man with a cane
She cuddles so close she never looks away
Many try to catch her eye not a one will today
They walk pass her window then bend for a view
Phil in the blue suit tries tying his shoe
Still she stares straight ahead not a glimpse of her eye
As the 7:40 Syosset to New York quickly races by
Some rustle their papers and books page by page
Reading the stories that today are the rage
Tomorrow as always everything will again change
Leaving today to the past with its stories of fame
Still cuddled so close not an inch can you see
The golden-haired beauty sits focused to be
Put to command as she learned while in school
This four-legged wonder that's nobody's fool
If ever a man needed love by his side
This Golden Retriever is the one to reside.

WOLRAD/2000

FINDING LOVE

*The following Reason happens after the story. I wrote this
part first, then wrote the story. It's so sad that I couldn't put
the ending in the poem. It's a story I came up with one day
while watching people wandering through a small outdoor
market in Ontario, Canada.*

*Dad, did I ever tell you how Sarah and I met
Ted began telling the story to his wife's father
As they stood together in the first row
No son, but Sarah did
She thought you a little crazy that day in the market
Yet she saw something fascinating in you
I guess that's why she married you so quickly
I loved her with all my heart Dad
I would run down to the market at lunchtime
Just to bring her a card with a lover's rhyme
We talked for hours every day
The world was special for us that way
I can't believe she's gone
Forever I won't see her face
Except in my dreams*

"Your melons are beautiful and those Vidalia's!"
Rolled from my lips so quick
She must have thought me crude and thick
To say out loud as if my schtick
An answer from her lips I'd wish to kiss
Without a question from this Miss
Her market just a stand so small
Gave the appearance that she was all
Alone no ring or thing appeared
Just long and curly lovely hair
Is this love or lust I feel
How can someone like me know it real
Or fake or what is it that makes
My knees give way this day
As not before I'm frozen here
The summer's warmth won't thaw away
What I can feel right here today
My heart or is it my inner mind
That says give it a try
Her answer may be no or why
Still I must give her the chance to be
Beside me just for lunch or tea
Could what I feel be love not lust
I must or soon I'll just go bust
"Miss, may I ask you a question?"
Blurred from my lips

"Surely sir!" She said
I paused I froze
I wondered if my clothes
Were short or long down to my toes
I bent my head to see
When I looked up her eyes so blue
Made putty out of me
"I am impressed with your market that is
And I'm interested in those plums
If only I weren't all thumbs
Which I'm not most of the time
But you have knocked me off my feet you see
Would you have lunch some day with me?"
I thought I'd die a million deaths
How could I be so rude
This lovely dream in jeans and boots
Could she have ever understood
Then a smile broke out and she said "Yes!
Why not you seem so nice
I'll pack your fruits and other things
In these brown paper bags
And write my number on this tiny tag."
She started wrapping my mind said slower
No hurry now that I
Had the chance to date this kindly beauty

My wish came true should I question why
I thought to myself not a word came out
It's too easy to find love this way
I picked up my bags and said "Goodbye
I'll call you in a day."
So many thoughts ran through my mind
She seemed so nice so kind
My ego sent the urge to call
My heart pumped I won't judge at all
My brain began its indecisive way
To screw up all my dreams that day
I called and she said when and where
We picked a place out in the air
The lunch was all I could ask of He
Each gesture each word said this is how love should be
We planned again and again to date
Before I knew it we set the date
The wedding and our families
Added to what was before just a family tree
Life was all I could ever want it to be
All the love in the world wrapped around me.

                              WOLRAD/2000

WHY NOT EAT WORMS

I was sitting one afternoon and watching a couple of Robins that return each year in Spring. They must have four nests that they have built over the years, under my deck. Each spring they pick and choose from the nests they have built and move right in. They are like family to us.

I got to thinking...do Robins have a relationship with mice? And if they did, what would their conversation be like. As you will see, I added a wise old Owl to the story.

Why not eat worms
Said the Robin, the beauty of the farm
To the Mouse who'd never caused him any harm
A worm to me means life you see
It gives me strength to fly and to be
As free as a bird can ever be
That's why the worm means so much to me
The Mouse replied in a squeak and a sway
I could not eat a worm in that way
Or any other I suppose on any other day
A nut, some seed would fill my tummy
Or from that tree I'll search for honey
Above so perched you could hardly see
A wise old Owl announced "Why not ask me?"
The Robin jumped to a branch nearby
The Mouse looked up to the two in the sky
With a hoot the Owl began to agree
A worm at times is tasty to me
And I enjoy a nut from that old nut tree
Then the Owl jumped off his branch so quick
The Mouse just froze as stiff as a stick
He moved so fast as he shouted loud with a squeal
"A Mouse is my favorite kind of meal!"

WOLRAD/2000

SCARED SILLY

I was driving on a road in eastern Pennsylvania when I saw a bear crossing, just a few yards in front of me. I looked at her as she gazed at me. I was wondering what was going through her mind. I felt safe in my car, though it did give me the shivers. Such a beautiful animal. In a way, I wanted to make some kind of contact with her.

When I got home, I sat down and wrote this rhyme as if I crossed paths with a bear while walking in the woods.

There she stood with mighty claws
Insides growling for some more
Her great shadow cast over me
As the biggest old oak tree
Would she let me live and pass
I thought as this massive lass
Leaned towards me her breath so warm
Went right through me like a thorn
I won't look or move or think
She can strike me in a blink
Then I'll bleed from all my veins
In this moment I'm insane
Full of fear as not before
Since Ma whipped me for ducking chores
When she caught me at the door
I don't duck them anymore
Please forgive me I say deep
Not a word from me or peep
I shall go down a brave soul
Please I'll pay you any toll
It was as she knew my drift
She turned and as if a precious gift
Walked away in her slow way
Moving all that blocked her way
I will never take for granted
All what I have wanted for
I will think of life romantic
I won't ever want for more
And when the bear within the stars
Comes down to take me there
I will welcome her in knowing
She let me live these many years.

WOLRAD/2019

SWAN LAKE

I belong to a New York City club called The Dutch Treat Club. Most of our members come from entertainment, fine art and writing careers. While attending one of the many Tuesday lunches, I sat next to a lovely woman who painted for a living.

I mentioned I would often write a poem that fits the painting or photo that friends and family have shown me. I took her card and looked up her work on her web site. I was extremely impressed with her paintings of Swans on a lake.

I wrote the following rhyme and emailed it back to her. Her return note said she was thinking exactly what my poem implied when she painted the piece.

I can hear their sounds so softly
The white Swans that glide about
I can see the lotus blooming
As they juggle for some clout
I'm in that dream where I'm alone
The scene is cloudy without rain
I sense the water's motion
I'm deep within and there's no pain
Will I wake and be much wiser
As this dream has once again
Brought me closer to a heaven
From this place where I pay rent
My eyes for just a moment blink
Where is this place I cannot think
Bring me back I ask for one more view
I promise I'm not sure to who
I wake the morning's filled with light
I've dreamt my way throughout the night
I watch in awe the morning sky
White clouds against the blue roll by.

WOLRAD/2019

BECAUSE

I was walking in the woods near my home lake house in Pennsylvania when I noticed the Evergreen trees. They never drop their leaves in fall. There's a kind of turning of the pines that takes place.

As I walked along, I was thinking about retirement and why people of retirement age still hold on to their past.

These are the days we rest our weary minds
Like the Pines that slowly turn and wait for Winter
They have not the leaves to cover the ground around
To warm the earth within its path
We question is this our last Winter
Have we lost our way this day of Fall
Have we forgotten what life is like and what little time is left
To spoon in June and eat ice cream in Summer
Have we forgotten our days when they were long
Has our song been sung and our words no longer spoken
Are we broken and without repair
Have we ceased to care
Have we no longer the hunger to be fat with ideas and wants
What taunts us is only a lust for what we have known
What reminds us daily are the days we have grown
What limits us are the ones who say enough is enough
Those comments so tough for those of us beyond our days
We have known the ways
We have paid the price
We have spent the time
So why are we here holding on to what was
Because…?

WOLRAD/2018

I JUST GOT BIT

I don't have to tell you how it feels to be bit on the butt by a mosquito or a spider while you are sitting outside having a nice lunch with friends or family. Well, that's exactly what happened to me. And, more than once, may I add.

I was enjoying one of those great big fat hot dogs I get from my butcher, Hebrew National, of course. When a mosquito bit me on the butt, I jumped off my chair and went after the critter. I could never figure out how they can disappear so quickly. Well, this one did and left his welt on my behind that I scratched for the next few days.

I had to put down on paper what this experience was all about. I am sure you will feel the itch just as badly as I did.

A bug just bit my bottom
I was sitting at the time
I must have sat down on him
In the space I thought was mine
It itched a bit
I must admit
I put lotion on to heal
That little insect bit
Who's seat I thought to steal
I never found that little flea
Or fly or what its name could be
It went off to its hiding place
So fast in its quick moving pace
The next time that I need to sit
Upon my outside chair
I'll look to see
If that old flea
Is lingering right there
I'll flip and check it everywhere
This time I'll take the time to care
And when I'm sure there's nothing there
I'll place my derriere.

WOLRAD/2018

REFLECT

What strange things we recite to ourselves at different moments in our lives. How often have you asked yourself a question while looking in the mirror? We always seem to be reflecting back as pupils in a classroom.

I can recall having a little too much to drink one night. As I went to brush my teeth and get myself ready for bed, I saw myself in the mirror. I kept moving from side to side trying to get out of the way of the image in the mirror. I could not believe, at that moment, I was looking at myself.

The next morning, I still had that image in my mind. This is what I came up with to reflect what I was feeling.

As you look in the mirror
And see what was and is
Look closely and
   Reflect
There are images not yet seen
There are moments to still sing
There are many thoughts and dreams
   Reflect
There can be moments you've tried
There can be words that you hide
There are those times you did not abide
   Reflect
When can you find true peace
When will your mind release
When will you sign that final lease
   Reflect
Can time erase what was
Can you succeed because
Can she/he make up the cause
   Reflect
You search down deep within your mind
Though you may look back to find
What was and can't be redefined
   Reflect.

WOLRAD/2018

THE RACE IS ON

Who knows what pops into your head at times? I see many of my thoughts as rhymes. I like this style of rhyming the last word of a line with the first word of the next line. I feel a strong punctuation is needed, though as you can see, I don't punctuate my poems. I leave that to the reader,

At the end of the fifth line; "elude your space...next line...Race!" I can't tell you where this flow comes from. It's one of my styles, or formats if you will, that seems to always work, in my mind anyway.

I believe I was contemplating retiring when I realized how much of a gift time is. I have written an opening line many times in my poems, that I've yet to use in this book. It goes; "If time would stand still just this once...then..." I'll leave this one for you to finish.

Is not each moment a precious gift
I ask of you this day
Is not the time we spend a blend of all our thoughts
Caught up in the rage of events that never pause
Cause not these moments to elude your space
Race towards them it is not to be disgraced
Place garland upon the head of those in need
Feed their souls with more than food
True love is the way to give them pride
Don't hide away in some lost place
Your case may never come to pass again
When you rise each morn be there
Not where you are not
Or where you feel you don't belong
Your song is still a tune unsung
Shown in the light you are the one who sees
Free that wish that moves you to another place
The race is on.

WOLRAD/2018

CAREFUL YOUNG HEARTS

I was watching a TV show that had a brief amount of nudity with a scene that reflected a great deal of lust and love. I thought how easy it is to fall into a place such as this. How easy it is for the lust to overcome you.

Though what consequences will follow once you take someone to your bed and make love with, she or he. The obligation changes. A commitment would seem a logical path to follow. Then you wake up the next morning, or even immediately after making love, and you are not sure.

How often have you, as I, found yourself in such an embarrassing predicament?

Careful fool heart of your belief
She stands there with her words a thief
To steal away your heart this day
With wants the same as you she says
Your feelings are as not before
Your heart pounds hard that closed locked door
Desire in the silence whispers clear
This is true love shed now your fear
As dark the room her breasts shine bright
You will have her and she you this night
You can't turn back or look away
For love has found you both today
You share as you've not shared before
Your heart's desire more and more
The night ends with the brightest day
Each one in your own loving way
Looks back at what last night has cast
Is this the love through life will last
You hold each other as close you can
She is your woman and you her man.

WOLRAD/2019

MY DREAM

Dreams, what can I say? You love them and you hate them. They sometimes, almost all the time, go on for your entire life. You hear your spouse talking in her sleep. Your children wake up screaming, to tell you that a giant monster was running after them.

Then all too soon, you forget, until the next night when the same dream returns.

I do not know or even try to comprehend
What lingers from my dream this night past
Yet still there is a feeling that I wish to lend
For just awhile I pray the memory still lasts
Dreams are peculiar to say the least
They feast on the day's events
Often waking you in a cold scary sweat
That haunts you till once again you sleep
There are those times we choose to remain
Deep within that moment as we rest
The test I've found asks the question
As I mention what leaves me cold
The older dreams forever live in corners to repeat
Past stories that live deep within my sleep
At times I may win to then lose quick
In darkness the black is so thick
As with the whale "it beckons me!"
I question "why must it be?"
I awake I start my day the same old way
Once more the dream and I no longer fight
Until I sleep to dream again tonight.

WOLRAD/2018

RESOLVE

We all reach that moment in our lives that we must resolve an important issue. It may be family related or not. It may be a romance or just a friend that hasn't been your friend of late. Many things change the position people want to be in.

Thank goodness we have that someone to ask for help or blame when you need. He or she is always there waiting to hear. At times we may bend a knee, other times we just scream it out. In any case, our fears and concerns need at one time or another to eventually be resolved. This sonnet attempts to reflect those feelings.

I shall not lose myself in my resolve
For I have wakened much from deep within
There is no choice we all must give to solve
Or suffer greatly from what wrongly sins

Our reasons are not chosen often sent
By our own family and our dear friends
We may again bend knee and ask repent
As fears will surface and new times will trend

Are these the voices that we hear inside
Or are they memories of days long gone
We can go on or we can try to hide
It's our own destiny must judge us wrong

We who are filled with desire and of want
Let us now count our blessings and move on.

WOLRAD/2018

BEFORE I CLOSE MY EYES

Often, I would sit on a bench I've set up near the brook that runs beside my home. I was writing about my thoughts, when it came to me, just how much I love my wife.

It was summertime and the flowers and trees were bursting with everything they can produce. I let my mind wander into these words about love and spring and the summer day.

I am without the thought of Spring
The sounds of birds their bellowing
The flowers that have just begun
To bloom again in the warming sun
I am without what could have been
As my heart goes a wandering
My love is here
That's all I care
I keep her always near
She is that spark that lights my day
She is my precious dear
Today the sun shines in the sky
The clouds are few they can't defy
As summer makes its rounds again
I search for words within my pen
Not easy not at all for these
Warmest days put me at ease
I'm pleased that's all I must admit
Feeling sharp and feeling fit
This night I'll walk that same old path
I'll praise with joy this day I've had
Then look towards he who makes things right
Before I close my eyes and say good night.

WOLRAD/2018

SEASONS

How many ways can we describe the seasons? How they change from year to year. This spring was rainy. I can't wait till this winter gets out of here, it's been so cold. Why must it be so hot this summer, and when it rains it pours!

I always try to find the finer things about the seasons. The beauty of the change of leaves when summer turns to fall. A snowfall, so slow and beautiful you want to count the flakes.

This is one of the many poems I've attempted, and always seem to fall a bit short, of when and how the seasons change.

Winter blows its way
The snow against our door
Spring brings forth its flowers
We hope will bloom forevermore
Summer melts those miseries
That tease at us each day
Till Fall appears
Leaves disappear
The trees are once again so bare
It's Winter's turn as was before
To pile the snow up to our door
Within the flames that warm our core
We shall not want for less or more
For soon what was a season
With all its changing heartfelt reasons
Leaves with promises that declare
I shall return once more next year.

WOLRAD/2018

FAMILY

I've always felt, coming from a family of four kids, living in The Bronx in a small apartment with one bath, that family is the most important part of life. Who else can you depend on? Things seem to be changing in our modern world. Comes the holidays, you can hardly muster enough family to have a nice dinner. If it wasn't for people dying, you may never see some of your cousins.

It must be the times. Years ago, your uncles and aunts lived nearby. They were always coming over for one reason or another. If your parents couldn't watch you, they sent you to grandma or an aunt. There was always lots of family around. When kids go to college today, they never seem to find their way back home. It's nothing for a child to move to another state because of work or to start a new life with someone.

I'm not sure we should have given up "the old days" so fast. The new days leave a lot to be desired, especially all those great old meals at my grandmother's house.

We gathered at least once a year
Then some disappear as if
A Piper led them off a cliff
Now there are those chosen few
Who stick together like the toughest glue
Without for the slightest reason
Stay in touch throughout the seasons
For them it would be treason
They sigh and say
They were brought up back in the day
Their blood flows true the old-time way
They will always keep in touch
Dependable in a clutch
For their family still means so much
Whichever they be it's like history
Some make it to the pages of fame
Then some will revoke
As if never they spoke
A word or played any game
Their pages are blank
As if always outflanked
Who can guess how they were spawned
They go their own way
Day after day
To never know a bright sunny dawn
I've known every kind
They don't bother my mind
I still love each one the same
For where would I be without my family
Those who carry my forefather's name.

WOLRAD/2018

DON'T HIDE

How often do you get those heartbreaking calls at night? A good friend of mine just couldn't get his act together. I promised him I was going to write a poem and email it to him that night. This is what I wrote to him. He is still constantly in the dumps. I wish I could come up with the words to break him free from his life-long depression. I won't give up.

Why do you hide
Where do you go
How do you know
If they're your friends or foes
Why search for something so hidden it's lost
Along comes the suffering at a very high cost
Rise from those shadows
Come out from the dark
Sit by a tree and carve into its bark
Leave all that sorrow
Take a breath for the pain
Look towards the sunset
Don't hide in the rain
Tomorrow will be there
With you or without
Show them you still can muster that clout
Let go of what haunts you
Rehearse a new part
The role won't be easy
Take sail with new charts
Then wake to a new day
My good friend please try
If not it's for sure
You'll soon say goodbye.

WOLRAD/2018

IS THERE REALLY MORE THAN THIS?

How often we ask ourselves; "Is there really more than this?"
When we start out, the questions about life begin. As we get
older, the questions change. The older we get, more questions
(though fewer answers), seem to be there. We tend to torture
ourselves with why this and why that? This poem is a reflection
of those many questions through life we seek answers to.

Is there really more than this?
That first encounter that first kiss
The beauty of a bright sunrise
Those holiday gifts you were so surprised
The first time you had to lie
So many tearful last goodbyes
All that life gives and some that you've missed
Is there really more than this?
You try to remember your first step
All those dreams each night you slept
The hurt within you've kept
How hard you worked each time you schlepped
Those quiet moments you cherished
Is there really more than this?
At times you reached so deep to find
What you have stored in your mind's mine
There wasn't time to do those things you missed
Is there really more than this?
You must know while you still draw breath
Before your death are you remiss
You want what some you trust promised
Is there really more than this?

WOLRAD/2018

SOMETHING
SPECIAL

I was sitting in a restaurant just across from the cutest little toddler. She was playing with her food as children do, yet she was well behaved. I thought how special she was. As I often do, I made a note on a piece of paper and later wrote this reflection of that moment and what it meant to me.

When you look at something special
    like a painting on the wall
Like a sunset at the end of day
    as the sun begins to fall
Like the snow in dead of winter
    as the flakes land softly on the ground
Like a child that just won't smile
    with the cutest kind of frown

When you look at something special
    that sets your heart to beat so quick
Something you can almost taste
    like candy on a stick
Something that amazes
    like a slick magician's trick
Something that your mind records
    like a Technicolor flick

When you look at something special
    like that glow that fills her eyes
As she sends out all that love you feel
    it makes you want to cry
Like the ocean with its soapy waves
    that pounds all night and day
To capture all its secrets
    in the deepest darkest caves

When you look at something special
    can you say the same for them
What they perceive as special
    may not be your chosen gem
For life stores its special moments
    just for you to find some day
When you look at something special
    it will never wash away.

WOLRAD/2015

I LOVE MY FATHER SO

*I've written many poems for a local Pennsylvania newspaper,
The Hideabout. To date they total about sixty. I've yet to miss
a publication in five years.*

*On various holidays and occasions, I write something that
fits the occasion. This is the Father's Day poem from 2015.*

He toots his horn in his own way
At times a little loud
I would not know him if some day
He became part of the common crowd
His younger years he was a Pro
The cards flipped as they do
Boxing was his best he told me so
He even knocked out a chosen few
As times changed he soon became
The builder of new dreams
This was for him the biggest game
Creating strong forever lasting scenes
So many kids would call him Dad
Four totaled our small clan
He's mine and I'm so proud and glad
He's led our family band
So again on this Father's Day
I'll brag to all I know
I've said it here in my own way
I love my Father so.

WOLRAD/2015

ARE WE REMISS

*I spend so much time walking the streets of the great city of
New York. I've certainly become aware that the subway system,
though problematic at times, is the only way to get anywhere in
a reasonable amount of time. I'm sure if you asked the average
streetwalker or subway rider, they would agree that so many
people seem to have their hand out. Possibly more than ever
before.*

*I'm not saying it's because they are homeless or because
they have drinking or drug problems, I'm just saying there are
so, so many unfortunate people that walk our streets during the
day and have no place to lay down at night. During the winter
months it seems even more obvious when such unfortunate
people are compelled to sleep with corrugated cartons around
them just to keep from getting frostbite.*

*I know there are shelters that the city has created for these
unfortunate citizens. I know that there are soup kitchens to help
many of them get a hot meal. I also know we are remiss if we
believe that our city and our more fortunate folks do enough
about it. These are some of my feelings in verse.*

Are we remiss
When asked why
And have no answers
Are we remiss
When someone dies
And we could not cure the Cancer
Are we remiss
When those in need
Are lost and we don't share
Are we remiss
When those who live by greed
And we don't care
There's so much more
To all those what's and why's
That meets the eye
Sometimes we cry
Sometimes we look the other way
Are we remiss
Today?

WOLRAD/2019

WHY DO I LOVE THEE?

So many poems ask the question; Why do I love thee? I've written a few verses over the years trying to capture the thought in that moment. I must admit with a topic so easy to write to, I've been stumbling at times to find just the right words.

I wrote this to my wife on a Saturday morning. It was the first day of Passover and the day before Easter Sunday. The weather was rainy with the promise to clear up by noon. I wanted so much to make this version my best ever.

I did like the way it came out, though I will try again, I'm sure, to find that perfect way to say; Why do I love thee?

Besides the closing rhyme and reason on the following pages, I wanted this to be my final poem in this, my first poetry book.

Why do I love thee?
If you ask I'm remiss
For not saying I love thee
Since we shared our first kiss
How not may I love thee?
When the night haunts me with dreams
Scenes of you lying here
Our hearts saying
    "Is this what love means?"
How long may I love thee?
There's no clock that chimes when
The love that we cherish
Will never grow dim
Why have I loved thee?
Please don't ask me my sweet
Without you and I touching
I would not ask life to repeat
There are so many riddles
That linger for years
Puzzles without pieces
Full of misguided tears
We've resolved many riddles
Our puzzle's nearly complete
No one said it was easy
We dug deep with our cleats
You ask…
"Why do I love thee?"
Without you by my side
I'd be just a stranger
With nowhere to hide.

WOLRAD/2019

IN CLOSING

If you've made it to this final closing page, I thank you for your time and patience. I hope you have enjoyed reading My Rhymes for Reasons.

I know, as well as any poet, that my words are written as a reflection of me. They are my expression of a moment that I must, for who knows why, share with others. I am compelled to write and reach out at every chance. The true reward is the joy my work brings to those for whom I have written my many rhymes, poems and short stories.

If I ever may write that one piece that fills my heart with what I've been searching for, I promise, you will be the first to know. Until then, I will continue to scribble on every piece of paper, napkin, the open areas of magazines and any other white space that I deem needs to be filled.

I leave behind my thoughts
In verse with pen
Reflecting back those many whys and whens
From memories of just today and long ago
I write with open heart so you will know
These notes left folded in my many books
Rewritten for you upon to look
To see my thoughts my ways my dreams
That I have painted with my pen of so many scenes
If I not be allowed again to be in print
I leave you My Rhymes for Reasons
So you recall my short stint.

WOLRAD/2019

www.ingramcontent.com/pod-product-compliance
Lightning Source LLC
Chambersburg PA
CBHW020730250626
47155CB00006B/2234